Published in the United States by Random House Children's Books,
a division of Penguin Random House LLC, 1745 Broadway, New York,
NY 10019, and in Canada by Random House of Canada, a division of
Penguin Random House Ltd., Toronto. Random House and the colophon
are registered trademarks of Penguin Random House LLC. Nickelodeon,
Teenage Mutant Ninja Turtles, and all related titles, logos, and characters
are trademarks of Viacom International Inc. and Viacom Overseas Holdings
C.V. Based on characters created by Peter Laird and Kevin Eastman.

randomhousekids.com

ISBN 978-0-553-52275-4

Printed in the United States of America
10 9 8 7 6 5 4 3 2 1

TEENAGE MUTANT NINJA TURTLES

MUTANTS IN SPACE!

Adapted by David Lewman

Based on the teleplays
"Annihilation: Earth! Part 1," "Annihilation: Earth!
Part 2," and "Beyond the Known Universe"
by Brandon Auman

RANDOM HOUSE 🏠 NEW YORK

CHAPTER 1

Late one night, the backstreets of New York were quiet and empty. A dim streetlight flickered. Nearby, an engine broke the silence. *VROOM . . .*

A strange vehicle came around a dark corner. It looked like an old subway car that had been converted into a makeshift military truck. Someone had spray-painted the name Shellraiser on it.

Inside the Shellraiser were two humans . . . and four Teenage Mutant Ninja Turtles.

Leonardo was at the wheel. Raphael was ready to fire the Shellraiser's trash cannon and manhole-cover launcher, if necessary. Michelangelo was navigating . . . sort of. Mostly, he was thinking about getting pizza at the end of the night. As chief engineer, Donatello was adjusting controls, ready to make any necessary repairs.

The two humans were the Turtles' best friends, April O'Neil and Casey Jones. The Shellraiser only had four seats, so April and Casey stood, holding subway-type straps.

Donnie did not look happy. "Guys," he said as he stared into a view screen, "someone's been following us for the last five blocks or so."

April frowned. "That's weird. I don't sense anyone at all." April's psychic powers usually alerted her when other living beings were nearby.

"See for yourself," Donnie said, gesturing toward the screen.

The others leaned forward and saw a black sedan following them as they turned another corner.

Whoever was driving the car didn't even bother to hide the fact that he was tailing the Shell-raiser. It was as if he knew the Turtles were on to him. He came up behind the Shellraiser, practically touching its back bumper. The sedan pulled past

the Shellraiser, and the Turtles got a good look at the driver.

"It's the Kraang!" Casey cried.

Casey was right. The driver of the black sedan was an alien Kraang in a fake human body. The Turtles had seen plenty of these disguised Kraang, and they all looked the same: black suit, black hair, and dark sunglasses.

But as it drove past the Shellraiser, this Kraang did something they'd never seen one do before. Smiling, it put its hand to its sunglasses, lifted them, and rapidly closed and opened one eye.

"Did that Kraang just *wink* at us?!" Raph asked, surprised.

The black sedan sped off into the night.

"After him, Leo!" Donnie shouted.

Leo hit the gas. The Shellraiser was gaining on the sedan when it suddenly disappeared.

"In there!" Mikey directed, pointing. "He turned into that alley!"

Leo took a sharp right turn into the alley. It was a dead end.

The Turtles opened the doors of the Shell-raiser and jumped out, followed by April and Casey. They looked around, but the black sedan and its mysterious winking driver were nowhere to be seen.

April spotted something on the brick wall in front of them. "Check it out," she said. "There's something written on this wall!"

"In New York alleys, there's *always* something written on the wall," Raph said.

"Yeah, but I think this is a message for you guys," April said. She read the writing out loud: "TURTLES. 3117 BAYFRONT STREET. MIDNIGHT."

Mikey pointed to a drawing below the writing. "What's that supposed to be? His logo?"

Leo examined it more closely. "It's a chess piece. A bishop."

The Turtles stared at the drawing. A bishop? What did *that* mean?

Just before midnight, the Turtles arrived at the address written on the alley wall: 3117 Bayfront Street. It turned out to be a meatpacking plant.

The Turtles, April, and Casey hopped out of the Shellraiser, keeping quiet. All their senses were sharp.

They looked around, but all they saw were a few people in the distance and a homeless man sleeping on the street.

"For the record," Raph growled, "I still think this is a terrible idea, Leo. Gotta be a trap."

Looking up at the meatpacking plant, Mikey realized something. "Dudes, this is the same meat warehouse where we fought Tiger Claw! Come on, I know a back entrance!"

He hurried around the corner of the building. The others followed him.

This is good, Leo thought. *The Kraang won't expect us to come in this way, so maybe we'll get a chance to check him out before he knows we're here.*

Cold sides of beef hung from metal hooks. The Turtles, April, and Casey made their way from one to the next, hiding behind the meat as they snuck deeper into the building, until . . .

. . . there he was! The winking Kraang from the black sedan! And he hadn't noticed them. They crept closer. Leo held his finger to his mouth, signaling the others to keep silent.

But Casey Jones wasn't very good at following orders.

To Casey, when you saw a Kraang, you did one thing and one thing only: attack!

"GOONGALA!" Casey howled as he leaped forward, swinging his hockey stick at the Kraang. "Goongala" was his new battle cry, and he was

hoping it would catch on. Mikey had "booyaka-sha." Shouldn't Casey have a trademark, too?

WHIFF! The stick missed its target as the Kraang leaned back, smoothly dodging Casey's blow.

"Casey, stop!" Leo cried.

His warning came too late. *WHAM!* In one swift motion, the Kraang swept his leg around, kicking Casey to the ground.

So much for the element of surprise. Now that Casey had started a fight, the Turtles had no choice but to jump in and help their friend. "Get him!" Raph yelled to the others.

Raph got to the Kraang first, but his ninja skills proved no match for the Kraang's. *WHOOMP!* With ease, the Kraang took Raph down.

"Do not do this," the Kraang warned.

But Mikey was already leaping toward the alien. "I got him, dudes! *YIIIAAAHHH!*"

Mikey swung his *nunchucks* at the Kraang, but the alien swiftly trapped his hands, took away his *nunchucks,* bopped Mikey with a fist, and smacked him with his own weapon.

"UGHHH!" Mikey groaned.

"Mikey!" Leo called, concerned that his brother was hurt. He drew his *katana* sword from its sheath strapped to his back and attacked!

But the Kraang moved so fast that Leo couldn't get anywhere near him with his sword.

"I am not here to fight you," the Kraang said.

"Too late for that!" Leo answered, drawing his second *katana* sword and swinging both of them wildly at the alien. The Kraang dodged every blow of the swords so rapidly that he became a blur.

"That's imposs—*OOOF! UGHHHH!"*

The Kraang had landed a single mega-fast punch to Leo's chest that sent him sailing back through a row of hanging sides of beef. This Kraang might have *looked* like all the others, but he sure didn't *fight* like them!

Seeing his brothers so easily defeated didn't stop Donnie from entering the battle. Without hesitating, he jumped toward the Kraang, whipping his *bo* staff right at the alien's head.

"YIIIIAAAAAHHH!" he cried as he attacked.

But the Kraang blocked the *bo* staff, shattering it! He grabbed Donnie, pulled him close, spun him around, and locked him in his grip.

The other three Turtles stared at the Kraang, shocked. He had Donnie!

The Kraang held Donnie tightly in his grasp.
Donnie struggled, but there seemed to be no escape.

"Turtles!" the Kraang said sharply. "Refrain from attacking! Believe me when I say *I am not your enemy.*"

He let Donnie go. This Kraang was different from any he'd ever seen. It seemed . . . almost human.

April tried to use her psychic ability to read the Kraang's intention. "I sense he's telling the truth. He's not like the other Kraang. I think he's one of the good guys."

A Kraang who was one of the *good* guys? Leo, Raph, and Casey weren't ready to believe it. Not

yet. They stood ready to resume the fight the second the alien showed any sign of aggression.

"You may call me by my Earth name," the Kraang said. "Bishop."

"Ah," Mikey said, nodding knowingly. "And when you wrote that note on the alley wall, you drew a bishop! Coincidence? I don't think so."

"But you look just like all the other Kraang!" Casey protested, not ready to be friendly with this alien.

"I was the one who created this body," Bishop explained. "The other Kraang copied me."

He opened up his human body, revealing the Kraang alien body inside. The small, brainlike creature looked peaceful.

"I am a member of the Utrom tribe," he continued, "a small group of Kraang defectors. We broke away from the Kraang Hive Mind many centuries ago."

Donnie nodded, looking very interested in this piece of information. Even in a tense situation, he loved learning something new. "Fascinating. It makes sense the Kraang share a hive mind. A really *stupid* hive mind!" Then he realized what he'd just said. "Um, no offense . . ."

Bishop closed his human body, hiding himself inside again. "I have broken my Utrom vow not to intervene in earthly matters, but I must warn you: *the Triceratons are coming.*"

The Turtles, April, and Casey couldn't believe it. They'd just recently fought a single Triceraton alien and beaten him, stopping him from sending a signal beacon into space. "The Triceratons?" Leo gasped. "As in *plural?* But we *stopped* the beacon!"

Bishop shook his head. "No. They are coming, and they are carrying enough firepower to destroy the entire solar system."

Mikey gulped. "Could you repeat that last part?"

"The news gets worse," Bishop went on. "The Kraang have finally fixed the Technodrome and are about to invade once more."

The Turtles couldn't believe it. *The* Technodrome? The Technodrome was the Kraang's huge and deadly weapon, an enormous spaceship with terrifying firepower. The Turtles thought it was lying at the bottom of the ocean, broken.

"Do you have any more terrible news, Bishop, or is that it?" Raph growled.

The alien turned toward Raph, fixing his stare on him. "If the Triceratons arrive when the Technodrome rises from the sea, they will home in on this planet and vaporize it."

The Turtles, April, and Casey looked totally freaked out. "Sorry I asked," Raph said.

April stepped forward. "Bishop," she asked, "why do the Triceratons hate the Kraang?"

"For millennia the two species have fought over Dimension X," Bishop explained, walking over to a table. He took a small device out of his pocket, placed it on the table, and pressed a button. A holographic image appeared above the device: Triceratons battling Kraang on the floating islands of Dimension X. "The Kraang used their intelligence to battle their foe, while the Triceratons relied on brute strength and cunning."

The holographic image shifted. In space,

Kraang Technodromes shot powerful laser blasts at Triceraton raptor fighter ships and a huge Triceraton mother ship. The Turtles stared at the miniature battle, fascinated.

"It seemed the Triceratons would win," Bishop said, "but the Kraang used the most powerful weapon in the universe. . . ."

"Sarcasm?" Mikey guessed.

"A black hole generator."

In the holographic projection, an immense weapon generated a black hole.

"It wiped out the Triceratons' entire planet."

The tiny planet was sucked into the miniature black hole with a *POP!* The Triceraton mother ship was surrounded by Triceraton raptor fighters.

"Only a single Triceraton fleet of spaceships survived. They vowed vengeance against the Kraang, at whatever cost."

Bishop pushed a button and the holographic projection vanished. "The battle may have ended, but the war still rages across Dimension X."

Everyone stared silently, awed by what they had seen. Then Leo spoke up. "Why are you helping us, Bishop?"

Bishop cocked his head, as though he were slightly puzzled by his own actions. "Because . . . I have watched you. I have seen the good you have done in quiet, in *secrecy,* simply for the sake of goodness. *That* is why I help you. Now . . . shall we begin?"

Deep below the streets of New York, in an abandoned subway station, the Turtles lived and trained in their lair with their father, Master Splinter. Splinter stood in the doorway of Donnie's lab, reassuring Leatherhead, a fierce mutant who had started life as a pet alligator.

"Do not worry, Leatherhead," Splinter said in his calm voice. He gestured toward Slash and Doc Rockwell. "They are still asleep. They will heal in time, but they need rest."

Slash, a massive mutant who had begun life as a pet turtle, was bandaged up. Doc Rockwell, also known as Mad Monkey, a brilliant scientist who had mutated into a giant monkey with telepathic powers, had an ice pack on his head. Both had been injured fighting the Triceraton.

Leatherhead looked as grateful as a large, mutant reptile could look. "Thank you, great Splinter, for caring for my friends."

The Turtles, April, and Casey entered the lair's common room, bringing Bishop with them.

"We're back, everyone!" Mikey sang out. "And we've brought a new pal!"

When Splinter and Leatherhead saw Bishop, their mouths fell open. Leatherhead was instantly so furious that he sounded like a mighty engine revving up. "Kra . . . Kraaaa . . . KRAAAAANNNNGGG!"

"No! No, wait!" April cried, trying to stop him from attacking Bishop.

Too late.

Leatherhead swung his arms and snapped his jaws at Bishop. But the Utrom Kraang dodged the mutant reptile's attack just as easily as he had the Turtles'. Within seconds, he tripped Leatherhead and slammed him to the ground.

"Leatherhead! Calm down, dude!" Mikey said. "It's okay. This is Bishop. He's a good Kraang! An Oolong!"

"Utrom," Donnie corrected his brother. "He's not like the others!"

"I do not trust him," Leatherhead growled, staring at Bishop.

Leo assumed his role as leader. "All right, here's the plan. Raph, Donnie, Mikey, and Leatherhead—you take the Sub. Infiltrate and stop the Technodrome underwater, before it launches. But if it *does* launch, the rest of us will take it out from the Turtle Blimp."

Splinter looked concerned. "The *Technodrome*? Leonardo, what is going on here?"

"There's no time to explain, Sensei," Leo said. "You just have to trust me when I say the whole world is at stake—and only we can save it."

CHAPTER 5

At the bottom of the bay, deep in the cold seawater, sat the Technodrome, stuck in the mud. Inside, on the bridge of the gigantic flying weapon, Kraang Subprime was excited. The Kraang's second-in-command and master spy still wore the robotic disguise he'd worn when he went undercover as Irma, April's friend from school. But the disguise was open, revealing the alien inside.

"Finally!" he cried excitedly. "After two Earth-years of repairs, miscalculations, and general mess-ups, the Technodrome is ready to fly again! *Voilà!*"

Using his tentacle instead of a robotic arm,

Kraang Subprime pressed a button on a control panel. The Technodrome started up, sputtered, and died with a metallic wheeze.

Kraang Prime, the leader of the aliens, glared at Kraang Subprime, annoyed. "What is that which is known as the *problem,* Kraang Subprime?"

CLICK. CLICK. CLICK. CLICK.

He kept pushing the button, but the Technodrome kept sputtering, failing to start up. The purple face of Kraang Prime scowled even more than usual.

High overhead, above the bay, Leo, April, Casey, and Bishop floated slowly through the sky in the Turtle Blimp. They were tracking the Turtle Sub below the surface.

"All right," Leo said. "Let's hope Raph's team can take down the Drome."

"And if they cannot," Bishop added, "we must destroy it. *At any cost.*"

They looked at the explosives rigged to the

carriage of the Blimp. Casey smiled, always happy to see anything blow up, but April wasn't so sure about their plan. . . .

Below the waves, the Turtle Sub swam through the water, diving down toward the Technodrome. Donnie was driving. When he'd gained enough distance from the gigantic weapon, he powered the Sub down.

Raph, Mikey, Donnie, and Leatherhead launched themselves out of the craft and swam to the Technodrome. None of the Kraang saw their approach. With his massive strength, Leatherhead tore a hole in the side of the metal Drome and the four of them slipped through. . . .

Back on the bridge, Kraang Subprime's button-pushing was growing more frantic. "Don't worry, oh Heinous One!" he said to Kraang Prime. "Kraang Subprime will get this baby started in two shakes of a tentacle. Heh . . ."

Suddenly, an alarm sounded! *VREEE! VREEE! VREEE! VREEE!*

"NOW WHAT?" Kraang Prime thundered. "Why is this not Kraang Prime's day? WHY?!"

In a corridor of the Technodrome, the alarm blared as Raph, Donnie, Leatherhead, and Mikey ran, fighting throngs of Kraang as they made their way through the shiplike weapon. Raph spotted Kraang aiming a huge cannon at them. "Leatherhead! Take that cannon DOWN!"

Roaring, Leatherhead leaped toward the cannon, toppling it just as it fired! *FWOOM!* Mikey and Donnie were busy knocking down more Kraang.

"We gotta get to the core!" Donnie yelled. "MOVE!"

Battling the Kraang, they made their way down the hallway. . . .

On the bridge, Kraang Subprime was still punching the ignition button over and over. "Come on, come on . . . ," he muttered, panicking.

Finally, the Technodrome hummed to life!

"YES!" he cried joyfully. "Sweet Mother of Kraang!"

"The Technodrome . . . RISES!" Kraang Prime announced in evil triumph.

Up in the Turtle Blimp, Leo, April, Casey, and Bishop watched as the surface of the water began to boil. Then . . . *WHOOSH!* The gigantic Technodrome emerged, dripping, from the bay, and rose into the air!

"Oh, no," April said in a small voice.

"That is just so awesome!" Casey exclaimed, "and *terrifying*."

CHAPTER 6

The massive Technodrome rose, higher and higher. It was so gigantic that it made the Turtle Blimp look like a kid's birthday balloon.

Leo yelled into his T-phone. "Raph! You guys have two minutes to blow that thing before we do!"

Raph's voice crackled through the T-phone. "Back off, man! We're heading to the core now!"

Back on the bridge, Kraang Prime proudly looked at a monitor that showed the Technodrome hovering above the Earth's surface. "Excellent work, Kraang Subprime! Now to mutate the WORLD!"

A Kraang-droid approached Kraang Subprime. "Kraang Subprime, that which is known as a balloon is heading for that which is known as—"

"Just spit it out already!" Kraang Subprime barked impatiently.

"Okay, *look!*" the Kraang-droid said, pointing at the monitor.

Kraang Subprime turned just in time to see the Turtle Blimp flying straight into the side of the Technodrome with all the explosives strapped to its carriage!

"You gotta be *Kraanging me!*" he yelled.

BOOM! A huge explosion rocked the Technodrome.

Outside, Leo, April, Casey, and Bishop sailed through the sky wearing glider wings. They aimed for the massive hole they'd just blasted in the side of the Technodrome.

"I told ya it wouldn't be enough to bring down the ship!" Casey cried. "Casey Jones knows explosives!"

Leo led the way toward the hole. "That wasn't the point, Casey! We just need a way in! And we've got it!"

They sailed through the hole into a giant corridor. Immediately, they were in a fight with the Kraang. Leo hurled *shurikens* while Bishop blasted away with his lasers.

Bishop kept cool under fire. "Hopefully, Raphael's team will reach the core without being disintegrated. Most likely not."

"You're such an optimist!" April observed.

The four of them dropped their glider wings and continued on foot, running deeper into the ship.

In a different part of the Technodrome, Raph, Donnie, Mikey, and Leatherhead found themselves surrounded!

"Turtle and alligator mutants," a Kraang-droid ordered, "you will raise that which is known as forelimbs."

They had no choice. They raised their hands.

CHAPTER 7

Meanwhile, Leo, Bishop, April, and Casey were running along a corridor, taking down Kraang as they went. Leo used his *katana* swords to slash two Kraang-droids. Casey battered another with his bat, while April used her *tessen* fan to deflect laser blasts.

"Where to, Bishop?" April shouted.

Using his incredible martial arts moves, Bishop wiped out five Kraang-droids in four seconds flat. He dusted off his jacket and adjusted his crooked sunglasses. "This way," he said calmly.

He raced off. Leo, April, and Casey followed. They stopped suddenly when they spotted Raph,

Donnie, Mikey, and Leatherhead on a level below them.

They were prisoners.

With their weapons drawn, Kraang-droids escorted Raph, Donnie, Mikey, and Leatherhead onto the bridge.

Kraang Prime and Kraang Subprime were waiting.

"This plan just keeps goin' south," Raph muttered.

Kraang Subprime flashed an evil grin. "Well, if it isn't the Turtles and that stupid alligator thing that shouts 'Kraang' all the time! Looks like he's not shouting now!"

High above them, Leo, April, Casey, and Bishop were watching. They had managed to stay out of sight so far. Leo was waiting for the right moment to attack the chamber full of Kraang and rescue the others. If the right moment ever came . . .

"Welcome, Earth Creatures!" Kraang Prime sneered, gloating over his prisoners. "You are about to enjoy that which is known as the *invasion of Earth*!"

He and Kraang Subprime burst into sickening laughter. Raph was about to say something defiant when another alarm sounded! *VREEE! VREEE! VREEE! VREEE!*

Kraang Subprime looked furious. "What now? Seriously? *Again?!*"

He ran over to the monitor to see what was going on outside the Technodrome. What he saw amazed and appalled him: the Triceraton mother ship flying close to the Earth's moon!

Kraang Prime was shocked, too. "The . . . the . . . Triceratons? Here? *Now?*"

"No, no, no, no, no, NO!" Kraang Subprime cried. "Not the Triceratons! Not here! Not NOW!" He flailed his tentacles in the air, frustrated at this maddening turn of events.

On every monitor aboard the Technodrome, a hulking Triceraton with a broken horn, a scarred face, and a steel beak appeared. His cold eyes stared out from the screens for a moment. Then he spoke. . . .

"Greetings, Sub-Life-Forms of Earth. I am

Captain Mozar of the Triceraton Empire."

Who you calling sub-life-forms? Mikey thought. *Also, what are sub-life-forms?*

Captain Mozar didn't take over just the video screens aboard the Technodrome. He could be seen on TVs and cell phones all over Earth. Some people stopped on the street to watch him on TVs for sale in shop windows.

"Let it be known," the Triceraton leader continued, "that your planet is infested with Kraang, an insidious alien bent on mutating Earth into their own home world."

On the bridge of the Technodrome, Kraang Prime and Kraang Subprime bared their teeth, snarling with anger. "Infested"? "Insidious"? "Mutating Earth"? Well, actually, that last part was accurate.

"In response," Captain Mozar said, "we Triceratons will eliminate these hideous aliens, freeing you from their vile plans."

In the Teenage Mutant Ninja Turtles' lair, Splinter intently watched the Triceraton's speech on a TV. He knew the Triceratons were formidable enemies. Stopping them wouldn't be easy. . . .

"Unfortunately, your Earth will be annihilated as well. That is all. And please . . . have a nice day."

The screens went blank.

All over the world, people screamed in terror!

On the bridge of the Technodrome, everyone was stunned by Captain Mozar's description of the Triceratons' plan to destroy Earth. Even Kraang Prime and Kraang Subprime.

"Holy chalupa," Donatello gasped. "It's actually happening! *Double invasion!*"

In his hiding place high above the bridge, Leo decided this was as good a moment as any to make their move—while all the Kraang were standing there with their mouths hanging open. "Let's do this, Bishop!" he hissed.

April, Casey, Leo, and Bishop leaped down, swinging into action. *"GOONGALA!"* Casey yelled. While he, Leo, and April knocked out

Kraang-droids, Bishop jumped right onto Kraang Subprime!

"Get off my robo-back!" the alien screamed.

Bishop punched Kraang Subprime, but the alien used his robotic arms to grab Bishop and throw him off his back. When he saw who had attacked him, Kraang Subprime yelled, "Bishop? You filthy, swindling Kraang!"

"Takes one to know one!" Mikey shouted. He thought that was a pretty good crack.

"I am an *Utrom*!" Bishop answered, springing to his feet, ready to fight. "Just as you once were, brother! Or shall I call you *Sub*-Subprime!"

Kraang Subprime looked livid. "Don't call me that! You know I hate that!" He activated the saw blades on his Irma-bot armor and attacked! *"RAAAAHHHH!"*

Bishop dodged the whirring blades, shouting to the Turtles, "Hurry, my friends! Get to the hangar!" He moved toward Kraang Subprime, ready to fight.

"Thanks, Bishop!" Leo said. "Let's go!"

When April, Casey, and the four brothers

were back together, Raph said gruffly, "Took ya long enough!"

"Whatever, dude!" Casey said. "Now . . . *how are we going to get out of here?*"

"Especially with *that* in our way," April added, pointing.

Kraang Prime roared and slammed his huge tentacles down on the ground, narrowly missing the group. *WHAM!*

"You go *nowhere*!" he bellowed.

As Kraang Prime moved toward the Turtles and their human friends, Leatherhead leaped up and smashed Kraang Prime in the face! Startled, the oversized alien staggered back.

"I'll hold it off!" Leatherhead shouted. *"Go!"*

Leatherhead clamped onto Kraang Prime's massive face. Flailing his tentacles, the alien fell back into the wall, smashing control panels and sending sparks flying!

The Turtles hesitated to leave Leatherhead behind. But Donnie knew they needed to get out of there. "Move it, guys!"

When they reached the hangar, Leo led the way to a row of stealth ships. "It's too late to blow this thing!" he said. "Pair up and grab a ship!"

Mikey joined Casey in a stealth ship. They immediately took off. Donnie and April paired up in another ship—Donnie was always happy to be paired up with April. They whooshed out of the hangar.

That left Leo and Raph together.

Leo fired up the ship's ignition and blasted out of the Technodrome just as a platoon of Kraang-droids arrived and started shooting their lasers at the fleeing Turtles!

CHAPTER 9

The Turtles flew the three Kraang stealth ships away from the Technodrome, quickly putting as much distance as possible between themselves and the flying weapon.

They'd have to worry about the Technodrome later. For now, the Triceratons were their biggest concern. Destruction of the Earth took precedence over mutation of the Earth.

On their view screens, the Turtles saw a squadron of five Triceraton raptor ships flying in attack formation.

"They're not just targeting the Technodrome," Leo said as he steered the stealth ship. "They're heading for the city!"

He and Raph watched as the Triceraton raptor ships branched off and flew past the Statue of Liberty!

"Then push this thing faster, Leo!" Raph barked.

In the sky above New York's harbor, the Turtles' stealth ships rocketed to intercept the five Triceraton fighters. Inside the raptor ships, the Triceraton pilots grunted the strange guttural sounds that made up their language.

They'd spotted the Turtles—and they recognized the ships as belonging to the Kraang, their mortal enemy!

BZZOOF! BZZOOF! BZZOOF! The Triceratons fired their energy cannons right at the Turtles' ships!

Leo hit the controls, and they managed to swerve out of the way at the last second.

The other two stealth ships were having problems of their own, with the raptor ships firing repeated blasts at both of them. All three stealth ships were in an incredible battle with the five Triceraton fighters!

Mikey and Casey streaked by and zapped a raptor ship. Below them flew Donnie and April's ship. They were dodging and firing with careful and precise aim, using April's psychic ability to pinpoint the Triceraton raptors.

"Over there!" April called out. "That way! Now four o'clock! That way—eleven o'clock!" By calling out the positions of numbers on a clock, April was telling Donnie precisely where to steer the ship.

"We make a pretty good team!" Donnie said, grinning. "Even though the odds of us surviving this are 967 to one!"

April hit the weapons control, blasting a Triceraton raptor!

"*Yes!*" she cried excitedly. "This is *too awesome*!"

Donnie shot her a look. That language sounded uncomfortably familiar. "You've been hanging out with Casey *way* too much!"

Mikey and Casey had a completely different style of aerial combat. They flew their stealth ship wildly, spinning and spraying laser fire in every

direction. Amazingly, they were disabling Triceraton fighters right and left!

"Check me out, dog!" Mikey yelled. "And Sensei says video games are useless! How else could I learn to do this? *WOOOOO!*"

Leo and Raph swept past the Technodrome. On their view screen, they saw Leatherhead and Bishop leap out a window into the ocean.

Smiling, Raph said, "They made it! But the Technodrome's still flying."

Leo wiped his brow. "Not for long, it's not! Look!"

A squadron of Triceraton raptor ships zoomed toward the Technodrome and blasted it with a punishing barrage of energy! One shot grazed Raph and Leo's stealth ship, but they slipped away undamaged.

The Technodrome unleashed a massive counterattack on the Triceraton raptors. It looked as though the Drome could prove too much for the fighters. One of its shots hit Donnie and April's ship!

Panicking, Donnie cried, "We're going down! Grab on to something!"

Without thinking, April grabbed Donnie. A smile flickered across his face, until he realized they were gonna die!

"AAAAAHHHHH!" they screamed.

Their ship spun out of control, diving straight toward the roller coaster at Coney Island!

CHAPTER 10

CRASH! The ship smashed through the roller coaster. It hit the ground, skidded across the empty amusement park, and slammed into a carnival game.

Then it was still.

Nearby, Leatherhead and Bishop pulled themselves out of the brine onto a dock. Dripping wet, they spotted the crashed ship and ran over to it. Leatherhead wrenched off the bent door and tossed it aside.

"My friends!" he called. "Are you okay?"

After a moment, Donnie and April crawled out of the ruined ship, looking battered and dazed. "I've always . . . *hated* . . . roller coasters," April wheezed.

Overhead, two Kraang stealth ships streaked by, carrying Leo, Raph, Mikey, and Casey. April's T-phone rang. She pulled it out of her pocket and answered it.

It was Leo. He was on his own T-phone while Raph handled the ship's controls. "April, I need you and Leatherhead to get Splinter and the rest of the Mutanimals. Gather as many of our friends as you can."

In the stealth ship, Leo hung up his T-phone.

"What's the deal, Leo?" Raph asked as they flew by another ship.

"The deal is we're gonna need all the help we can get," Leo said grimly.

On the bridge of the Triceraton mother ship, Captain Mozar stared at a screen, watching the battle below. He did not look pleased. But then, with his face, it wasn't clear whether he could *ever* look pleased.

A Triceraton commander stomped up to him. "Captain Mozar, we have the Technodrome on target."

"Excellent," Captain Mozar said. "Destroy it. And unleash the Heart of Darkness upon the city. We will make sure the Kraang never take this world again . . . by *annihilating* it."

On the bridge of the Technodrome, Kraang Subprime studied a monitor and gasped. He quickly turned to Kraang Prime. "The Triceraton mother ship is powering up! We're toast! *Toast!*"

Kraang Prime slapped Kraang Subprime with his tentacle, sending his second-in-command flying. "Calm down, Kraang Subprime! Begin evasive maneuvers! Ready that which is known as the EYE OF KRAANG!"

Leo, Raph, Mikey, and Casey were still busy fighting Triceraton raptor ships. Other raptors were blasting the Technodrome with lasers. Then Casey spotted something.

"Mikey, look!" he cried.

The Triceraton fleet was backing off and scattering.

"They're leaving!" Mikey shouted. "YES!" But then he noticed something bright in the sky. "Uh-oh . . ."

The brightness in the sky above them was a plasma beam firing from one of the Triceraton mother ship's huge cannons. The beam streaked straight toward the Technodrome!

KAAAA-BOOOOOOOM!!! The Technodrome exploded!

The force of the blast sent Leo and Raph's ship flying out of control. Screaming, Leo and Raph bailed out!

Without a pilot, the stealth ship plummeted to the ground, rolled across the docks, and blew up! The noise was deafening! *BOOOOOOM!!!*

Raph and Leo fell through the sky. They had no glider wings. No parachutes.

But they did have grappling hooks.

They threw their hooks, catching the top of a billboard, and swung down onto a New York rooftop.

It was a hard landing. *WHOMP!*

The two Turtles rolled across the roof, battered and exhausted. Finally, they came to a stop and just lay there for a few seconds.

Leo's T-phone rang. Still groaning, he answered it. "Mikey?"

His brother's voice came over the phone. "Dude, there's a ship holding some kind of, like, energy string. It's carrying some kinda giant thingy!"

Leo frowned. "You're not making any sense, Mikey! What are you talking about? What 'giant thingy'?"

In their Kraang stealth ship, Mikey and Casey were peering at a view screen. They saw a Triceraton raptor with an energy tether trailing below it. Hanging from the tether was the Heart of Darkness, the Triceraton's black hole generator.

But Mikey and Casey didn't know what the giant thingy was.

Three more Triceraton raptor ships were guarding the ship with the energy tether and the Heart of Darkness.

Casey grabbed the T-phone from Mikey. "Looks like a weapon. Aw, crud! Guys, I think they're heading for Washington Square!"

Washington Square was a popular historic park in New York with a famous marble arch dedicated to George Washington.

"Take it down!" Leo ordered over the phone. "Whatever you do, *take it down*!"

That wouldn't be easy. There were four Triceraton raptor ships and just one Turtle ship. But Mikey didn't hesitate. He grabbed the T-phone back from Casey. "I got this, chief. Aw, *yeah*! Turtle spaceship power!"

Mikey swerved through the sky in a wild pattern, getting the raptor ship carrying the black hole generator in his sights. *"Fire!"* he yelled.

Casey hit the weapon controls, sending a blast toward the Triceraton ship. *"GOONGALA!"* he shouted joyfully.

Mikey couldn't contain himself any longer. He had to ask. "Dude, what *is* that?"

"My battle cry," Casey said. "It's really catching on."

"It's really not," Mikey said.

Their blast was timed and aimed perfectly. But when it got close to its target, it was deflected by a bubble that suddenly appeared around the ship.

"They have force field awesomeness!" Casey gasped, impressed.

"And, like, *four dudes blasting at us!*" Mikey shouted.

"There's too many!" Casey yelled.

BLAAAMM!

The Kraang stealth ship spun out of control, falling toward the streets of New York!

"MAYDAY! MAYDAY!" Mikey screamed. "WE'RE GOING DOWN, DOG!"

CHAPTER 12

The Kraang stealth ship wasn't very stealthy as it came screaming out of the sky. Struggling with the controls, Mikey was able to get the ship right-side up as it slammed into a side street. It skidded across the pavement, coming to a stop along the curb in a parking place right behind a tiny compact car.

The ship wasn't even damaged much. Apparently, the Kraang built their stealth ships tough.

"Whew!" Mikey sighed.

"Nice job, dude," Casey said. "I like the part where we didn't die."

They opened the door and clambered out of the spaceship.

Casey had been right about where the Triceratons were headed with their black hole generator. They dropped it in the center of Washington Square Park, right next to the fountain. With a solid *thunk.*

As soon as the black hole generator had attached itself to the ground, three Triceraton scientists beamed down from the raptor ship that had delivered the Heart of Darkness. Their ship flew off, and the three scientists immediately got to work arming the terrible weapon.

On the perimeter of the park, Leo and Raph arrived with Donnie and Bishop. When they saw the three Triceraton scientists working on the black hole generator, they ducked behind some bushes.

"What's going on, Bishop?" Leo whispered.

"They are scientists," he explained. "Their job is to program the black hole generator, which the Triceratons call the Heart of Darkness."

Leo grinned. "Scientists, huh? So they're not fighters. This should be easy."

He started to leave the bushes and head toward the three scientists, but Donnie put his hand on his brother's shoulder, holding him back.

"*They're* not fighters," Donnie said. "But those soldiers are."

Triceraton soldiers carrying blasters and plasma launchers had just beamed down from a raptor ship to guard the scientists while they worked.

"And they're armed," Donnie observed. "Heavily."

"Okay," Leo sighed. "We're gonna need the rest of the guys here fast. . . ."

They heard a familiar voice say, "Are we enough for ya?"

It was Casey! He and Mikey were sneaking up to join them.

Donnie noticed that the three scientists had stopped working on the black hole generator's controls. They looked satisfied with themselves.

Then the scientist who seemed to be in charge flipped one last switch, proclaiming, "For the Triceraton Empire!"

The moment the switch was flipped, the entire city of New York went dark.

"A blackout!" Mikey said. "What lousy timing! What're the odds?"

But Donnie instantly knew what was happening. "It's no coincidence, Mikey. The Triceratons are draining the city's energy supply to power their black hole generator!"

"All right, team," Leo said. "This could be our last battle. *Are you ready?*"

CHAPTER 13

Leo led the charge out of the bushes. They tried to run as quietly as possible but were quickly spotted by one of the Triceratons. "Earth creatures!" he growled. *"Attack!"*

"Take out their weapons!" Bishop called to the others.

Two hulking Triceratons rushed at Bishop, who swiftly dodged them, battering one of them. "I'll take the Triceratons," he told the others. "Go for the generator!"

Casey used his hockey stick to whack explosive pucks at a Triceraton's head, but the blasts barely slowed him down. He began to charge at Casey like an angry rhino!

Leo attacked with his *katana* swords, but the Triceraton's skin was much too thick. Leo might as well have been hitting the alien with plastic spoons. The Triceraton kicked Leo, sending him flying straight into the park's fountain. *SPLOOSH!*

Bishop was in constant motion, kicking, punching, and firing his energy gun. He was battling several Triceratons at once, and beating them.

Then Mikey saw a Triceraton aiming his weapon at Bishop from behind! "Bishop! NOOOOO!"

FWOOOM! The Triceraton fired his weapon, destroying Bishop's human body! The Utrom inside looked angry as he hopped out and scurried for cover, squealing.

Mikey ran right at the Triceraton who had shot Bishop, dodging his energy blasts, using his *kusarigama* chain to send the alien's cannon blasting at one of the Triceraton scientists. "Eat it, dinosaur!" he cried as he attacked.

The Triceraton was unfazed by Mikey's blows.

Mikey looked up at the beast looming over him and gave a little laugh. "Heh heh . . ."

As the Triceraton leveled his laser, taking aim at Mikey's head, the teenager closed his eyes and said quietly, "Goodbye, cruel world! Goodbye, delicious pizza."

Just as the Triceraton was about to pull the trigger . . . *WHACK! WHACK! WHACK!* Three *shuriken* hit his laser cannon, destroying it.

Mikey opened his eyes and saw . . . Master Splinter! He was standing right there in Washington Square Park, along with April, Leatherhead, Pigeon Pete, Slash, Doc Rockwell, Muckman, and Mondo Gecko! All the Mutanimals had come to help!

"We heard you might need some assistance," Master Splinter said calmly.

Leo, Donnie, Casey, and Raph picked themselves up off the ground, thrilled to see their sensei and their friends.

More Triceraton soldiers were beaming down into the park, all armed with energy cannons. They started marching right toward the Turtles and their allies.

Staring at the advancing soldiers, April asked, "So what do we do?!"

Mikey stepped forward, putting on his toughest face. "We kick their Jurassic! *Cowabunga!*"

He leaped toward the Triceratons, leading the charge!

14

The Triceratons saw the defenders of planet Earth running straight toward them. Their commander bellowed, "Triceratons! TEAR THEM APART!"

The Triceratons opened fire, but Mikey didn't slow down a bit. He hurled himself at the nearest Triceraton—who unfortunately was also one of the *biggest* Triceratons!

"BOOYAKASHAAAA!" Mikey yelled, whipping his *nunchucks* at the Triceraton. He got in a couple of hits, but the bulky alien swatted him away, knocking him to the ground.

Good thing turtles have shells. . . .

Raph and Donnie were busy dodging the

Triceratons' energy blasts. They saw even more Triceratons teleporting into Washington Square.

"They just keep beaming down!" Donnie cried. "We'll never get past them all!"

Raph whipped a handful of *shuriken* at one of the Triceraton cannons, disabling it. "We've got one thing they don't have—Master Splinter!"

As if on cue, their sensei leaped in and kicked another Triceraton, making it stagger back. Splinter landed close to Mikey and helped him up. "Stay strong, Michelangelo," he said. Then he turned back and called to the others. "Second wave! *Attack!*"

The Mutanimals didn't need any more urging. They were eager to fight these enemies. Roaring, they ran toward the Triceratons. "Mutanimals, ho!" Slash yelled.

Pigeon Pete, a mutant of both pigeon and human DNA, flew into action. But he got zapped almost immediately. Squawking, he landed in a pile of feathers.

"Pete's down!" Slash cried as he bolted into the fray. "Cover me, Leatherhead!"

He reached his friend and picked him up. Dodging laser blasts, Slash ran back to a safer area, where he carefully laid the Mutanimal on the ground. "Rest up, Pete!" he whispered. "I get the feeling there'll be plenty more chances for you to fight!"

CHAPTER 15

Casey sprang forward, batting explosive pucks right at the head of a Triceraton. They detonated, but the Triceraton stood his ground, glaring. The little bombs had only made him mad.

Behind his hockey mask, Casey's eyes widened. "Maybe I need an upgrade!"

Screaming like a wild man, Casey whipped his hockey stick around, whacking the Triceraton over and over. The furious Triceraton bashed him aside.

"Casey!" April screamed.

As the Triceraton loomed over Casey, April frantically looked around for a weapon. She spotted a laser cannon one of the Triceratons had dropped. It was so heavy she could barely lift it

LEATHERHEAD

This powerful Mutanimal was originally a normal pet alligator, but he was captured by the Kraang. Before he could escape, they conducted mutagen experiments on him, making him massive, strong . . . and angry.

SLASH

When Raphael's pet turtle, Spike, was accidentally splattered with mutagen, he became the super-powerful ninja named Slash. At first, he was violent and unpredictable, but eventually he gained self-control and joined the ranks of the Mutanimals.

BIOTROID

These gorilla-like robots are actually mechanical suits piloted by the Kraang. Massively strong, they are outfitted with saw blades that extend from their chests and explosive cannons in their butts.

MUTANTS IN SPACE!

ROCKSTEADY

He started life as a Russian arms dealer named Ivan Steranko, but Fishface and Rahzar captured him and threw him in a vat of mutagen. He was infused with the DNA of a white rhino and became Rocksteady. His parter in crime is Bebop.

BEBOP

Rocksteady's partner, Bebop, was originally a thief named Anton Zeck. He was captured while trying to steal Shredder's helmet and turned into a mutant warthog.

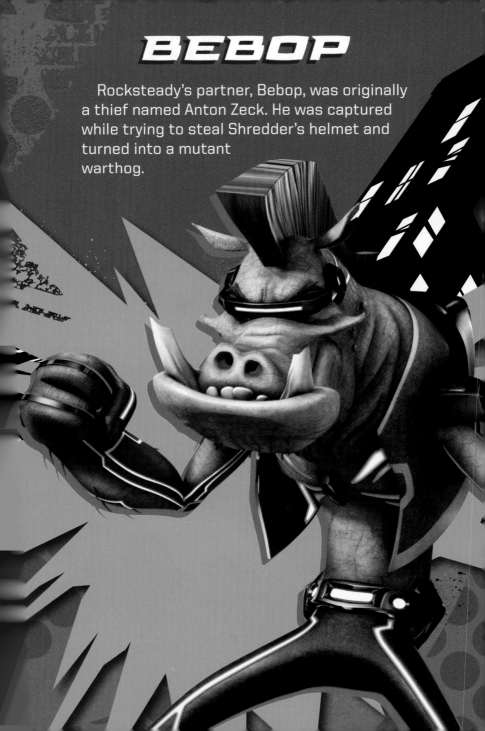

TIGER CLAW

This bounty hunter from Japan is a tiger/human hybrid. He began life as a circus performer, but after being mutated, he became one of Shredder's most dreaded henchmen.

with both arms, but she managed, and fired it right at the Triceraton threatening Casey. *BOOM!* The alien was sent flying back, but so was April from the force of the laser blast.

As Casey helped April to her feet, Mondo Gecko sped by on his skateboard. Flipping his board and making a fist, he yelled, *"Cowabunga! It's time for Mondo Gecko to open a can of—"*

WHOMP! Mondo Gecko ran right into one of the Triceratons. It was like running into the solid trunk of an oak tree.

Barely registering the impact of the mutant gecko, the Triceraton scratched his butt and turned around, seeing Mondo standing there, frozen. He and another Triceraton piled on, jumping up and down on the Mutanimal as if he were their personal trampoline.

Muckman, a mutated garbage man who looked like a pile of the garbage he used to pick up, saw the two Triceratons jumping on Mondo Gecko. "Mondo! *No!* Get away from my pal, ya alien freaks!"

Using all his strength, he picked up an over-turned car and threw it at the Triceratons, knocking them off Mondo Gecko. The Mutanimal had been seriously stomped on, but he was still able to groan. Muckman ran to his friend's rescue.

The Turtles and Splinter battled bravely, despite being vastly outnumbered by the Triceratons. More kept beaming down to join the fight.

Splinter saw that the Triceraton scientists were close to completing their task of programming the Heart of Darkness. One Triceraton scientist nodded to another, seeming to indicate that they were almost ready to deploy the awful weapon.

"We must stop the black hole generator from being triggered!" Splinter called to his fighting comrades.

Though he was busy deflecting laser blasts with his two *katana* swords, Leo heard his sensei. He in turn called to their two biggest, most powerful fighters. "Slash! Leatherhead! Take that machine down! *Now!*"

CHAPTER 16

That was all **Slash and Leatherhead** needed to hear. "Gotta trash that space gadget, Leatherhead!" Slash yelled.

"SPAAACCE GAAAADGET!" Leatherhead agreed.

Leatherhead hurled himself at the Triceratons guarding the black hole generator. As he fought them, he shouted to Slash, "I'll hold them off! You destroy the weapon!"

Slash made his way toward the Heart of Darkness, intent on bashing it with his spiked weapon. Swinging it, he knocked one Triceraton out of his way, sending him flying!

But two more Triceratons were headed toward

Slash. Doc Rockwell, a mutated monkey with psychic powers, saw that his comrade was about to be attacked!

"Oh, no you don't!" he yelled, picking up two cars with his telekinesis. He slammed them into one of the Triceratons. The other just kept on going, until Doc Rockwell used his mutant mind to lift him up and launch him over a building!

"Ha!" Doc Rockwell laughed. "Think you can withstand my vast telekinetic power?"

At that moment, a Triceraton landed right behind Doc Rockwell. He spun around, but before he could focus his thoughts, the alien yanked the helmet off Doc's head. Without it, the Mad Monkey couldn't control his telekinetic powers.

The Triceraton stomped on the helmet, smashing it to bits.

"NO!" Doc Rockwell cried. "You vile, extinct . . ." He was so angry he started screeching like an ape!

In his rage, the Mutanimal launched himself at the Triceraton, but the alien knocked him to the ground and tossed a glowing pink pyramid at him.

Doc Rockwell stared at the pyramid and covered his face with his arm, but the pyramid projected a force field bubble that captured him, lifting him off the ground!

With Leatherhead keeping the other guards busy, Slash had fought his way to the black hole generator. Roaring, he raised his spiked mace over his head and slammed it down on the metal device.

Nothing.

"Huh?" Slash said. He was used to seeing his mace reduce everything it touched to rubble.

He raised his mace again and again. *WHAM! WHAM! WHAM!*

If the black hole generator wasn't totally destroyed, at least it was damaged.

A Triceraton tried to stop Slash, but he knocked the

alien away with his mace. From the ground, the Triceraton tossed a glowing pyramid toward Slash—the same kind of pyramid that the Triceratons had used to capture Doc Rockwell. Slash raised his mace to smash it, but before he could swing his weapon, the pyramid projected a force field bubble that trapped him.

Leatherhead saw that Slash was captured inside the floating bubble. He ran over to the black hole generator and was about to smash it with his tail, when . . .

. . . Captain Mozar beamed down! He held a plasma cannon in one hand and a force field pyramid in the other. He hurled the pyramid at Leatherhead, trapping him in a bubble before he could attack the Heart of Darkness.

"Nooo! Triceratons!" Leatherhead roared inside the bubble. *"Let me go, alien!"* He slashed at the walls of the bubble with his powerful tail, but the force field withstood his blows.

Captain Mozar growled, "This battle is over! You have all lost!"

"Leatherhead!" Mikey yelled, seeing his friend trapped in the force field. Without thinking, he ran up a Triceraton, flipped off his back, and launched himself at Captain Mozar, spinning his *nunchucks*!

The Triceraton leader grabbed Mikey and lifted him into the air, kicking and struggling. "Foolish little one!" Captain Mozar sneered. "You are coming with me!"

"Mikey!" Raph cried.

Casey skated frantically toward Captain Mozar and Mikey, swinging his hockey stick. "I got you, dude! *RAAAAAH!*"

But before Casey could reach them, Captain Mozar pressed a button, activating a transporter. *SHWOOM!* He and Mikey disappeared, beaming up over the stone arch into the Triceraton mother ship! As they went, Mikey let out one last scream.

"Michelangelo!" Splinter cried.

CHAPTER 17

There was no time to think about where Mikey had gone, because at the same time Captain Mozar teleported away, many more Triceraton soldiers teleported in! They arrived in the park with their laser weapons aimed and started firing immediately!

Casey saw that they were now absolutely, *desperately* outnumbered! He turned and tried to skate away as fast as he could, but a Triceraton lobbed a force field pyramid right at his feet, capturing Casey in a floating bubble! *"YAAAH!"* he yelled, his screams muffled by the unbreakable walls of the bubble.

"Casey!" April cried. She ran toward the bubble, planning to free her friend . . . somehow!

"No, April!" Casey shouted from inside the bubble. "Run! *Run!*"

But April kept coming. Raph tackled her, pushing her out of the line of laser fire. "No!" he yelled. "April, you can't! It's too dangerous! There's just too many!"

April saw that Raph was right. As they ran, dodging plasma blasts, she called to Casey over her shoulder. "I'll come back for you!"

Now the firestorm of laser blasts was growing more and more intense. Leo tried to deflect as many of the blasts as he possibly could with his *katana* swords, but it was becoming far too difficult. If they stayed, they would surely die.

"We gotta go, Sensei!" Leo shouted to Splinter.

The rat master agreed. He gestured with his own sword, pointing away from the Triceratons. "Retreat!" he commanded. *"Everyone retreat!"*

They all ran, heading away from the Triceraton soldiers as fast as their feet could carry them. But as he ran, Donnie spotted something intriguing on a fallen Triceraton.

Hm, he said to himself. *This little baby might come in handy. . . .*

ZWOONK! A laser blast reminded him to keep running. *"YIAAAH!"* he yelled. But he still managed to snatch the object from the unconscious alien soldier before he went.

Nearly 100,000 miles overhead, the gigantic Triceraton mother ship hovered over the blue planet. On the bridge, Captain Mozar rematerialized with Mikey held behind his back, trapped in a force field bubble. Mikey was still screaming.

"Yaaah! Yaaaaah!"

Ignoring him, Captain Mozar strode across the bridge. Triceraton officers stood and raised their fists in a salute.

The last officer in the line was Mozar's second-in-command, Commander Zorin, standing with his back to his captain. He turned and raised his fist. Then he looked surprised and spoke in a voice made gravelly by years of screaming at underlings.

"Captain Mozar, sir! You have captured an Earth creature?"

Mozar gave a small nod, holding the force field bubble with Mikey inside in front of him for all to see. "A mutant species of some kind, rare to the planet."

Mikey struggled inside the bubble, hoping it might eventually pop, setting him free. "I used to think dinosaurs were cool! But not you guys!" He turned around in the bubble so he could face Captain Mozar. "Why are you doing this, dino-dude? Why can't you just leave Earth alone?"

The massive Triceraton leader glowered. "Why?" he snarled. "Because of the Kraang! We will not let them take this planet. They want it as a hiding place from Dimension X, a back door, where we Triceratons cannot detect them. So we will simply destroy your planet and all of the Kraang hiding there!"

Mikey desperately tried to think of an argument to make Mozar abandon his plan to destroy Earth. "But . . . but . . . *we* don't want the Kraang here, either!" He remembered a wise phrase he had once heard. "Can't we all just get along?" he pleaded.

"No," Captain Mozar said in a tone that showed there was no changing his mind. "The decision has been made by the Triceraton emperor. It cannot be changed."

While Mozar was talking, Mikey had formed his hand into a fist. He concentrated, calling upon everything Splinter had taught him, summoning all his energy and focusing it into one targeted blow.

"HIIYAAAH!" he shouted as he slammed his fist against the inside of the bubble. It gave way, and Mikey rolled onto the floor!

He jumped up to attack Mozar, yelling with rage! This dino-alien wasn't going to destroy his planet! Not if he could help it! "YAAAAHHHH!"

Mikey flew at Captain Mozar, determined to attack the hulking leader. But before he could even reach the Triceraton, Commander Zorin snagged him out of the air and held him fast in one huge hand.

Mikey struggled to get free. "Lemme go! Get offa me, dorkasaurus!"

Commander Zorin ignored Mikey's insult . . . but only because he was not familiar with the term *dorkasaurus.* "Shall I take him to the brig, sir?"

Captain Mozar considered this suggestion. Then he had an idea. He smiled—a cruel, cold smile. "No," he said in his deep voice. "Ready the Psionic Extractor."

The other officers on the bridge exchanged surprised glances, though they said nothing. They dared not speak up against Captain Mozar.

But Commander Zorin dared. "The Psionic Extractor? But, sir, we only use it on our greatest war criminals. It is too horrible and cruel even for the likes of—"

Horrible? Cruel? Mikey didn't like the sound of any of this.

"SILENCE!" Captain Mozar roared, leaning his face in close to Commander Zorin's. "Do not presume to lecture me on the use of the Psionic Extractor! I am well aware of its . . . effects. DO AS I COMMAND!"

Commander Zorin stared for a brief moment. Then he turned and nodded to one of the seated officers. The Triceraton pushed a series of buttons on the control panel in front of him.

A section of the wall opened slowly. A device resembling a chair bristling with blades and prongs emerged into the chamber. But it was no chair. It was the Psionic Extractor.

Sweating, Mikey nervously said, "Wow. Heh. That looks like it's really gonna hurt. Probably a lot."

Captain Mozar put his massive face right next to Mikey's. "More than you can possibly imagine, creature."

On a roof several stories above a New York City street, Splinter stood by a water tank. Leo, Raph, Donnie, and April were with him, hiding from the Triceratons, keeping to the shadows.

"We gotta go back for 'em, Sensei," Leo said urgently. "We can't just leave 'em there!"

Two Triceraton raptors screamed by overhead. The Turtles ducked out of sight.

"And what about Mikey?" Raph demanded. "What are they gonna do to him up there in that freaky ship? Probe him?"

Splinter looked grim. "I, too, am concerned about Michelangelo and the others. But first we must destroy the black hole generator. *That* is the priority. If we cannot stop this weapon, *the entire world is doomed!*"

"Sensei," Donnie said, "I think it's gonna take some time for the Triceratons to fix all the damage Slash caused. . . ."

"We gotta go after Mikey!" Leo insisted. "Even if we stop the black hole generator, we still have to get him back!"

Splinter leaped down from the water tower platform, landing among the Turtles. He thought for a moment. Then he spoke gravely.

"Go, then," he said. "Save your brother. April and I will stop the Triceratons and rescue our friends."

April looked surprised. "You and I? By ourselves?" She couldn't believe what Splinter was saying. "You're, um, kidding—right, Sensei?"

But Splinter didn't look as though he was kidding. He looked deadly serious.

"We will ally ourselves with someone even *more* powerful than the mighty Mutanimals," he said.

"Who, Sensei?" Leo asked.

Splinter closed his eyes, as though it was painful to state the answer out loud. "The Shredder."

April gasped.

CHAPTER 19

On the Triceraton mother ship, Mikey was strapped down, his arms held tight by thick metal restraints. The long, sharp extractor was pointed directly at his skull. He was trembling, though the cuffs severely limited his movement.

"Hold up, dino-dudes!" he squeaked. "Let's talk about this! For reals, though!"

"There is no need for talk," Commander Zorin scoffed. "This machine will drain all of your knowledge of Earth and the Kraang."

Captain Mozar leaned in, almost touching Mikey's face with his metal beak. "And in the process, your psyche will be sliced, diced, chopped, and removed from your puny brain."

"I don't have the biggest psycho," Mikey wailed, "but I like what I got!"

Mozar turned to one of the officers seated at a nearby control panel. "Activate the extractor!"

The officer pressed a button. Lights flashed. Ropes of energy crackled around the long extractor as it began to spin. It moved closer to Mikey's skull, focusing a triangle of light on his forehead.

A beam of glowing energy pulsed through his skull. Mikey screamed . . .

. . . but then his screaming turned to hysterical laughter!

"*BWAAH!* HA HA HA HA HA HA! WOW! YEAH! SO COOL!" Mikey laughed.

Captain Mozar's cruel smile turned to a frown.

Mikey kept giggling and laughing, kicking his feet in delight. He clearly was *enjoying* the Psionic Extractor, feeling no pain whatsoever!

"Turn it off!" Captain Mozar barked. "TURN IT OFF NOW!"

The officer hit a button. The machine powered down, releasing Mikey from his metal cuffs.

He sat up, his eyes wide, looking spaced out but happy.

"Dude! Why'd you stop?" he asked, lying on his back and kicking his feet in the air. "That was better than, like, a *hundred million* roller coaster rides through outer space!" Mikey jumped up and grabbed on to Mozar's horn, then got down on his knees and clasped his hands together, pleading. "Can I do it again? Can I? *Please?*"

"Shut up, shut up, SHUT UP!" Captain Mozar roared, furious. He wheeled on the Triceraton officer at the control panel. "What *knowledge* did you extract?"

The officer studied his console. "Very little useful information, Captain. The only thought the creature seems to have is for a substance called 'pizza.'"

"*Yeaaahh!*" Mikey cried. In his blissed-out state, he jumped on Mozar's leg, hoping for a ride. The Triceraton captain shook him off angrily.

Turning away, Mozar snarled, "Bah! DESTROY the pathetic alien!"

Commander Zorin grabbed Mikey roughly with one hand and tossed him back into the Psionic Extractor's seat. The metal cuffs slammed down on his arms.

"Whoa, whoa, hold up!" Mikey yelled. "I know stuff!"

"You know *nothing*," Captain Mozar snapped, still walking away with his back turned to the desperate Turtle.

Mikey had to think fast—as fast as he'd ever thought in his life. He blurted out, "I know all the secret bases where the Kraang hide in Dimension X!"

Mozar stopped in his tracks. He turned back and stared at Mikey. "Perhaps this creature *is* of some use to us. We shall see."

He started walking back toward Mikey, who was sweating, knowing his lie would only buy him so much time. . . .

Back on the surface of Earth, April ran from hiding spot to hiding spot, gradually making her way toward the entrance to Shredder's lair. Wearing a hood, Splinter appeared next to her, moving silently through the night.

"So we're actually doing this," April whispered. "Are you a hundred percent sure this is gonna work, Sensei?" She still couldn't believe they were going to try to form an alliance with Shredder, their greatest enemy.

Splinter glanced at her. "No one can ever be sure about anything, but that does not mean one should not try new things."

The rat smiled, but April was still extremely nervous about walking right into Shredder's lair and asking for help fighting the Triceratons. For

one thing, how were they going to get in?

Just as she thought this, a door creaked open a few inches. Odd . . .

Splinter looked wary but nodded to April. She slipped through the open door.

Inside the dark lair, April looked around. She saw no one, but then she heard footsteps! She opened her *tessen,* ready to throw the metal fan. Her eyes darted back and forth, trying to spot the source of the footsteps inside the gloomy hall. Suddenly . . .

. . . someone grabbed her arm! Dressed in full ninja gear, the figure had been invisible before it attacked April! "HAA HAAAA! Who do you think opened the door for ya?" the figure crowed. "It was me—*Bebop,* baby! Be to the *bop!*"

Splinter sprang into the chamber, knocking Bebop aside with his staff. *"AUUGGH!"* Bebop yelped as he fell to the ground in a heap.

Tiger Claw leaped down from the shadows, facing off against Splinter. "Bad move, rat! Breaking in here during an alien invasion? Are you desperate . . ."

He drew his blaster out of its leg holster and aimed it at them.

". . . or just FOOLS?"

BLAM! BLAM! BLAM! BLAM! Tiger Claw's weapon fired blasts of heat and cold at Splinter and April, who dove out of the way.

April sprang to her feet. "We're not here to—*whoa!*" She backed right into Rocksteady, a mutant member of Shredder's team of assassins who looked like a gigantic rhino!

"Ha! Is Rocksteady late for party time?" he asked in his Russian accent.

He grabbed for April, but she ducked out of the way, running between his legs to escape his grasp. She looked to Splinter for help, but he was busy avoiding Bebop's blast and kicking him away.

"Stop!" called a deep voice.

Shredder stepped into the chamber.

"I wish to know why Hamato Yoshi has come here," he said, referring to Splinter by the name he had gone by as a man in Japan, before he mutated into a rat. "Perhaps to end his miserable existence?"

CHAPTER 21

Splinter stood motionless between Shredder's blades and Tiger Claw's blaster. He spoke forcefully, without a trace of fear in his voice. "Our feud is meaningless in the face of this invasion, Saki." He chose to call Shredder by his old Japanese name, too. "The world will soon be destroyed. Will you sit by and watch? Or will you help us save it?"

Through a window high in the chamber, Shredder could see Triceraton ships streak by in the sky. But he ignored them. Instead, he held his blades close to Splinter's throat. "What have you done with Karai?"

Shredder claimed Karai as his daughter, having raised her since she was an infant. But in truth, she was Splinter's child.

Splinter looked down, pained by Shredder's question. "We searched for her, but she is gone. Alive, but vanished from the city."

SHINNNNG! Shredder shot the blades out of his gauntlet and raised them toward Splinter. "YOU LIE!"

April spoke up. "He's telling the truth, Shredder! Karai's still out there somewhere. And if the Earth blows up, guess what? You'll never see her again!"

April's eyes blazed, furious at the absurdity of Shredder's stubborn ways. "So maybe you can do the right thing for *once* in your evil life! Even be a *hero* for a change! That is, *if you still love Karai!*"

Shredder stared at April, stunned by her words. But he did not lower his blades from Splinter's throat.

On a New York street, Leo, Raph, and Donnie ducked next to a parked car. Carefully rising to the level of its windows, they peered through the car and saw a Kraang stealth ship wedged between two other parked cars.

"There's Mikey's ship!" Leo said. "Told you I saw it come down this way!"

"Wow, not a bad parking job, either!" Donnie said admiringly.

Hearing the Turtles' voices, a man and a woman who had been hiding in the car popped up and screamed! *"YAAAHHH!"*

Startled, the Turtles screamed, too! *"YAAAHHH!"*

"More aliens! Run!" the man cried as he slipped out of the car and scrambled away, followed by his terrified wife.

"Ugh," Raph grunted. "Humans are *so annoying* sometimes!"

The three Turtles hurried into the stealth ship.

Leo hit the controls and the ship came to life.

In just seconds, the stealth ship had broken free of Earth's atmosphere. Without gravity, the three Turtles floated around the inside of the ship.

Raph felt sick to his stomach. "Ugghhhh. Turtles were *definitely* not meant to go into space. . . ." As if to prove his point, Raph hurled!

"Hold on!" Donnie said, strapping himself into a seat. "Lemme turn on the artificial gravity!" He punched a button and his brothers fell to the floor. *THUMP!* Donnie laughed, until Raph's puke landed right on his head! *"AUGGHHH!"* he screamed, frantically wiping it off.

Leo looked out the view screen. "Guys, I see it! The mother ship!"

The other two looked up. And there it was, looming before them, the huge cone-shaped mother ship, guarded by several smaller Triceraton ships.

"Okay, but where's Mikey?" Raph asked.

"I'm detecting a unique life signature," Donnie said. "It's gotta be him! And check it out! I think I finally figured out the cloak on this baby!

Ha! They'll *never* find us now!"

Outside, in the bright light of the moon, the Kraang ship with its dangling tentacles, suddenly disappeared!

But the Triceratons were not fooled. . . .

On the bridge of the mother ship, Captain Mozar watched as Commander Zorin zoomed in on an image of the cloaked stealth ship, using high-tech imaging to render it visible.

"Idiots," Captain Mozar sneered. "They think they can hide from us. Tragic mistake."

He turned to his second-in-command. "Commander Zorin, deploy a squadron of fighters. Sergeant Zark, activate the plasma cannon!"

Outside the mother ship, four Triceraton raptor ships peeled off, flying toward the Turtles' Kraang stealth ship. The pilots looked as though they were enjoying the murderous task they'd been given.

On his screen, Donnie saw them coming. And that wasn't all he saw. . . .

"Okay," he said, his eyes widening. "This is disturbing."

Raph groaned. "Don't make me throw up again!"

A beeping from the control panel was getting faster and faster. *BEEPBEEPBEEPBEEP!*

"I think the Triceratons are locking on to us with their weapons," Donnie said.

The Turtles screamed as they swerved and weaved, trying to dodge the firestorm of laser blasts coming at them from the four raptors!

"HOW CAN THEY SEE US, DONNIE?" Leo yelled.

"Let me text them and find out," Donnie answered sarcastically. "I HAVE NO IDEA!"

A blast hit the ship! *"OOOF!"* the Turtles cried as they were thrown around the inside of the ship—which was now completely visible!

Leo took command, frantically trying to lose the four ships. "Raph! Man the defenses!"

"I'm on it!" Raph cried. He punched controls, sending blasts back at the pursuing raptors. *FWOOM! FWOOM! FWOOM!*

But the Turtles were taking more hits than they were dishing out. Finally, they steered right into one of the Triceraton ships! *WHAM!* Raph punched the control board over and over. Outside, the metal tentacle of the Kraang ship punched the raptor ship. A blast from a raptor knocked the stealth ship off. Raph fired a continuous blast until the raptor ship exploded!

"Aw, yeah!" Raph cried.

But there were still three raptor ships after them, and they were getting hit with more energy blasts than ever!

"We're not gonna make it!" Donnie cried. "There's just too many of 'em, Captain!"

But Leo grimly kept going, taking more and more hits from the raptors, energy crackling all around the outside of their craft.

Then, as the Turtles stared in horror, energy bands around the base of the mother ship started to glow. The ship rotated in space until its sharp tip was aimed right at the Turtles!

Donnie said, "I don't like the looks of—"

FWAAUUUGGHMMM! A huge blast of plasma shot toward the stealth ship. The Turtles screamed!

And in a blinding flash of light, their ship exploded!

CHAPTER 23

There was nothing left of the Kraang stealth ship. It was obliterated. Where it had hovered, there was only cold, empty space.

But seconds before the explosion, Donnie had grabbed his two brothers and hit the button on the device he'd taken from the fallen Triceraton back in Washington Square Park. *ZAAAAM!*

Inside the mother ship, the three huddled brothers beamed onto the bridge, still screaming. *"YAAAAHHH!"*

Donnie was the first to stop. He looked around and sighed with relief.

"We're alive!" Leo said. "We're . . . alive? How?"

Raph saw the object Donnie was holding. "You . . . you snagged a teleporter?"

"Uh-huh," Donnie said, nodding.

"You mean we could have just *beamed* here?" Raph shouted, outraged at all the trouble and danger they'd gone through when they could have just zapped themselves onto the mother ship.

"There's only one charge," Donnie explained. "And I—" He looked up. "Oh, man, we're in trouble!"

Armed Triceratons surrounded them.

In Washington Square Park, Triceraton soldiers patrolled the edge of the green, making sure no one came in to stop their scientists from repairing the Heart of Darkness.

Just for fun, one Triceraton passed a police car and casually punched it, sending it flying. *CRASH!*

On a low rooftop, another Triceraton watched for intruders. He heard a voice cry "Hoo hoo!" and whipped around, yelling "Halt!"

Above him, on another rooftop's water tank,

Bebop was waving. And dancing! He shook his hips. He pumped his fists. He moved his feet, all the while laughing. "Ah ha ha ha!" He even balanced on his head for a moment!

Holding his weapon in his arms, the Triceraton watched Bebop, fascinated. He even chuckled, amused by the Earth creature's dance. Then . . .

WHAM! Rocksteady punched the Triceraton, knocking him off the roof and onto a parked truck. *CRASH!* "Only room for one horn-head in these parts, cowboy," Rocksteady said quietly.

The sound of the alien crashing onto the truck alerted another Triceraton guard. "Huh?" he said, turning toward the noise.

But that turn, that small shift in his attention, was a mistake.

Shredder came out of the darkness, attacking with his blades! He sliced the soldier's weapon in half. The Triceraton managed to dodge his first few blows but then took a savage kick to the chest and was knocked unconscious.

"We must remain stealthy," Splinter warned in a low voice as he, April, Shredder, and Shredder's henchmen moved deeper into the park. To April's astonishment, Shredder had agreed to this temporary alliance. Maybe he really did love Karai. . . .

The group of unlikely allies slipped behind a parked garbage truck. April peeked around the corner of the truck at the Triceraton scientists working on the black hole generator. Then she pulled her head back and whispered to the others.

"Whatever we do," she said, "we'd better do it fast. I think they just fixed the timer on that thing!"

The others spied on the scientists, who looked pleased. One of them pressed a triangular button in the center of the timer. The countdown began. . . .

For once, Tiger Claw found himself agreeing with April. "We must not waste time, Master," he said to Shredder. "We must— Oh, no."

Even as the assassin urged haste, he saw that more Triceraton soldiers were beaming down into Washington Square Park. Two of the soldiers bumped massive fists.

Now there were

more guards to overcome if they were going to disarm the black hole generator! And they were already severely outnumbered. . . .

On the bridge of the mother ship, the four Teenage Mutant Ninja Turtles were reunited—as prisoners of the Triceratons. They were forced to kneel on the floor before Captain Mozar.

Donnie spoke in his most logical, convincing voice, "Captain Mozar, please. Don't destroy Earth! Our world has so much potential!"

Mozar glared at them. "The humans of the world are as thoughtless as the Kraang!" He pointed an accusing finger at them. "They pollute the planet and erode its ozone willingly, and they don't even need mutagen to do it!"

He turned to the guards. "Escort them to the air lock and be done with them!"

The guards grabbed the Turtles and roughly hauled them to their feet. Leo was the last on his knees. He stared at the floor, furious.

"You can destroy us, Mozar. That's okay . . . ," he said, controlling his anger.

Mikey looked at him, shocked. *"It is?"*

Leo raised his head and looked Mozar right in the eye, speaking with the utmost seriousness. "But I'm asking you one last time before I take this whole ship down: let Earth survive . . . or be destroyed!"

His brothers stared at him. They knew when Leo was telling the truth and when he was bluffing. This was no bluff.

"Empty threats!" Captain Mozar scoffed. "Get him out of my sight!"

A huge Triceraton guard reached down to grab Leo. But the ninja grabbed the guard's wrist, as thick as the branch of a tree, and whipped around it. As he fell back toward the floor, he snatched a teleporting device off the guard's belt. Landing on his feet, Leo took two steps, ready to hurl the teleporter at the wall of the chamber—an exterior wall, the only thing separating them all from outer space.

"What's this?" Mozar shouted. In a flash, he saw what Leo intended to do. "No! *Stop!*"

But Leo didn't stop. When he said he was going to take the whole ship down, he meant it. He hurled the teleporter at the wall with all his strength.

WHAM! The teleporter hit the wall and activated! *FFFFWOOM!* The part of the wall touching the device was beamed away, leaving a gaping hole.

The vacuum of space sucked everything in the chamber toward the hole—including Triceratons and Turtles!

The chamber was immediately filled with a roaring sound as air rushed through the hole. Several Triceratons were sucked across the room, screaming *"NOOOO!"* before they passed through the hole into the silent, deadly emptiness of space.

As the Turtles were yanked by the force of the vacuum, Leo grabbed a console. Donnie grabbed Leo's feet, Raph grabbed Donnie's feet, Mikey grabbed Raph's feet, and they all hung on for dear life. It was a Turtle chain!

But as Captain Mozar was pulled toward the hole, he grabbed Mikey's feet. Mikey desperately tried to hold on to Raph's feet, but the force of the flying Triceraton captain yanked him away.

"AAAAAAGGHHH!" screamed Mikey as he flew through the air with Mozar, heading straight toward the hole.

Captain Mozar was big enough to straddle the hole for a moment, facing the room with his back to the black void outside. That moment was just long enough for Raph to act.

"Mikey!" he called, whipping his grappling hook toward his brother. Mikey snagged the hook, and Raph pulled him free of Mozar's grasp.

As Raph hauled his brother away from Mozar, Mikey managed to snatch a device off his belt.

"Guys!" Mikey called, holding up the teleporter he'd snagged. "Check it out! *BOOYAKASHA!*"

The four brothers touched hands and activated the teleporter! *ZWOOPT!*

They disappeared!

"YAAAAHH!" The four Turtles hurtled through the air and landed on the ground, hard. *THWUMP!*

As they stood up, checking to see if they were all still in one piece, a plasma beam hit a truck next to them, blasting a huge hole through it. Mozar's teleporter must have been set for Washington Square Park, because they'd beamed right into the battle between the Triceratons and Splinter's forces!

And the battle was raging! The black hole generator's timer was ticking down, and Splinter's fighters still hadn't reached the Heart of Darkness.

The Turtles couldn't believe what they were seeing! April was fighting alongside Fishface and Rahzar! What kind of crazy alliance was this?

In the middle of the chaos, April slipped over to the force field bubbles where Casey, Slash, Rockwell, and Leatherhead were being held captive.

"April!" Slash called out, thrilled to see her.

"Red!" Casey shouted. "I knew you wouldn't leave us behind!"

"I'll get you guys out in no time!" April promised. She grabbed the small pyramid that was projecting Casey's bubble-cage. Kneeling down, she slammed it into the ground again and again, trying to break it so the bubble would disappear. "Come on, come on," she said, pounding it with as much force as she could muster.

Finally, the pyramid cracked and broke. The bubble popped, and Casey fell to the ground. He jumped up, free at last. "*Yes!* Thanks, April! You rule!"

They quickly hugged. Then April turned to the other three. "I'm getting the rest of you out!"

She picked up the pyramid projecting Doc Rockwell's force field cage. More Triceratons approached. Rockwell held up his hands inside the bubble, saying, "No! There's no time!"

A Triceraton fired his weapon at April, but Tiger Claw kicked his feet out from under him, sending his shot into the air. The assassin knocked the alien out and took cover. Then he turned to April and Casey. "Hurry, quickly! *Run!*"

April and Casey fled from the Triceratons' laser fire. The timer ticked down. There were only seconds left until the Heart of Darkness generated its planet-destroying black hole!

CHAPTER 26

Shredder threw himself at a group of Triceratons, punching and kicking, swinging his deadly blades through the air!

He knocked two down, but a third was about to shoot him from behind. Splinter ran to Shredder's aid, tossing blinding powder into the soldier's face. He staggered back, unable to see. Splinter dealt him several blows before another Triceraton rushed in, swinging his huge fists at the rat!

Splinter took on both guards at once, whirling and chopping, kicking and crunching the Triceratons until they had both hit the ground with a tremendous crash! One of the aliens fell right on top of Splinter. He crawled out and looked for Shredder.

"Hurry, Saki!" he called. "We have no time!"

He was right. The timer on the black hole generator had nearly counted down to zero!

Splinter rushed toward the device. Shredder was right behind him.

And then . . .

. . . long, sharp blades emerged from Splinter's chest!

Splinter groaned. Shredder had betrayed him!

Shredder pulled his blades out of Splinter, who pitched forward onto the ground.

The Turtles stood there in shock for a moment, frozen and furious. Then they started running toward their sensei. Their father!

April grabbed her head, unable to bear the pain of her grief and anger. *"AAAUUUGGH!"* She screamed with fury, throwing her arms wide and sending out an uncontrollable psychic blast that slammed Shredder, sending him flying across the park.

And the timer on the Heart of Darkness was still ticking down. . . .

Splinter's eyes slowly closed, and his heart stopped beating.

He was gone.

The timer ticked its last. The Heart of Darkness rose into the air, beginning to generate a black hole that sucked everything into it with an irresistible force.

Bebop looked up at the black device. "We're all doomed, dude! We are doomed! WE ARE DOOMED!" he cried.

Shredder leaned against the base of the fountain and smiled. He'd pulled off his mask, revealing his scarred human face. "Finally, Hamato Yoshi is finished!" He looked up, still smiling his cold, insane smile. "Earth can be destroyed, for all I care. I have finally won!"

The Turtles, April, and Casey ran to Splinter. Leo cradled his master's head in his lap. Mikey lay his head across Splinter's still body. No one said anything. What was there to say?

Casey saw a bright light shining down from above. A spaceship hovered over them. A door opened. A walkway extended from the ship to the ground. An inner door opened and a small figure stood silhouetted in the bright light.

It extended its hand and welcomed the Turtles, Casey, and April aboard.

Higher up, the black hole was growing, blocking out the moon. People gasped, staring up at it. Then they were lifted off the ground. The same teddy bear that was dropped on the street suddenly floated into the air and was sucked up toward the gaping black hole. People, trucks, buildings—the Earth itself was being pulled up into the black hole!

A hundred thousand miles up, the Triceratons watched triumphantly from their mother ship. Captain Mozar, who had managed to survive the hole in the side of the ship—and ordered it repaired—smiled. "Long live the Triceraton Empire!" he shouted, raising his fist in salute.

"Long live the Triceraton Empire!" echoed all the Triceratons aboard the mother ship.

The entire Triceraton fleet cloaked itself in invisibility and transported away.

As the black hole loomed over Earth, the small mysterious spaceship rocketed away from its deadly pull. "Everyone, hold on!" ordered its pilot.

The Turtles, April, and Casey held on, staring at a large view screen revealing what was happening to their home planet.

The small spaceship hurtled away . . . but not before they saw Earth disappear into the black hole!

CHAPTER 27

When the black hole swallowed Earth, a huge amount of energy was released, sending a giant shock wave across space! It rocked the small spaceship, sending everyone inside flying! *"YAAHH!"* they screamed.

Then, as quickly as it began, the shock wave passed over them and ended. Everything was eerily still.

The Turtles, Casey, and April looked up from the various spots around the spaceship where they had landed on the floor. April's eyes were huge. "Did . . . that . . . just happen?"

"Earth . . . Splinter . . . *everything* . . . ," Leo said.

"Gone," Donnie said. "Lost forever in an

infinite gravitational singularity."

"Holy pepperoni," Mikey said in a small voice.

The spaceship's pilot stepped forward. He seemed to be a robot or android of some sort. Speaking in a distinguished British accent, he said, "Watching your entire world vanish into the quantum singularity of a black hole *is* rather distressing. *Bloop bleep.* Can I offer you some hot cocoa?"

"Mm," Mikey said, accepting a cup and licking his lips. But then he looked up at the round-headed robot. "Dude. Who *are* you?"

"My name is Professor Zayton Honeycutt," the robot answered cheerfully. "And you, my friends, are about to embark on a wondrous adventure!"

The small spaceship rocketed off through the galaxy as the black hole devoured the rest of the solar system.

The only Turtle who hadn't spoken yet was Raph. But now he spoke. And he was mad. Very mad.

"Is that it?" Raph grabbed the robot by the neck and shoulder. "Is Earth . . . *gone*? This has gotta be some kind of sick joke! Right? *Right?*"

WHAP! Professor Zayton Honeycutt slapped Raph away. Then he grabbed his own head, as though Raph's anger had given him a headache. "Calm down, Raphael! First things first! I have a job to do!" He walked back to his control center and sat down.

Casey leaned in close to the robot's face, squinting, trying to peer into his small, round eyes. "How do you know our *names,* robot dude?"

Honeycutt pushed Casey back. "I know all about you, Casey Jones. Now, please. I've got a ship to fly while you all stand about gawking."

He busied himself with his controls, considering the conversation to be over.

But April got in the robot's face. "That's not good enough! Where are you taking us?" Who was this guy? If he knew so much, why didn't he care that these refugees had just lost their home, their planet, and the greatest mutant ever, Master Splinter?

"All questions will be answered in time." Honeycutt punched a button, and the ship began to vibrate violently. "Hold on to something!"

But the shaking was already too violent, and reality itself seemed to be coming apart! The Turtles and the humans started to scream!

"Oops—too late! Hold on!" Honeycutt said calmly. "Apologies! *Beep!*"

Mikey felt as though he were breaking up. "NOT . . . COOL . . . BRAAAAAH!"

But then they realized that the spaceship, and everything in it, was not shattering.

Something very strange was happening: it was going back in time!

The planets of the solar system spun past them backward! The black hole spat out Earth and disappeared! Earth whizzed through space backward through its orbit and then slowly settled into its normal rotation.

And then, things were peaceful.

"What . . . what just happened?" Raphael asked, kneeling on the floor. He touched his face and looked at his hands. "We're actually alive?"

Donnie stood up and stared out the huge view screen at Earth. "I think we . . . we went back in time. About six months, based on where Earth is in its revolution around the sun."

Professor Honeycutt walked up. "Impressive,

Donatello! You are quite the astronomer!"

Leo looked amazed. "Six months? Then that means . . . everyone's back? Including Master Splinter?" He grinned to think that his sensei was alive again.

The robot nodded. "Yes, Leonardo. But only for six months. And then Earth is doomed once more." He clasped his hands and hung his head. "Apologies."

April's face lighted up. "I get it! We stop the Triceratons before they ever get a chance to use the black hole on Earth!"

Raph nodded to Mikey, grinning. Now, this was more like it!

"Indeed," Professor Honeycutt said. "The Triceratons are spending this time searching the universe for the three fragments of the black hole weapon." He aimed his hand at the screen and said, *"Bleep!"* A light shone from his hand, and images appeared on the screen.

"Many years ago," he continued as an image of the black hole generator appeared, "the Utroms broke the black hole generator into three pieces."

The hoop on the screen broke into three arcs.

"They hid the three fragments in the safest parts of the galaxy they could find."

The screen showed the shining disk of the galaxy. The three arcs swooped into the galaxy, revealing the nebula and star systems where they'd been hidden by the Utroms.

"We must find them before the Triceratons find the fragments and reassemble them," the robot concluded.

Mikey chimed in. "And if we mess up, we just travel back again, right?"

Honeycutt shook his head. "No. A black hole prevents repeated localized time travel. Because even *time* is subject to its attraction! If we fail, Earth is lost forever!"

The Turtles looked at each other. "No pressure," Mikey said.

Casey still had a question for the robot. "So why do you care, alien robot dude? Why are you helping us?"

"I am a friend to the Utroms," Honeycutt answered. "It was Bishop who sent me. And I've always wanted to see Earth. Have I mentioned that I'm a scientist and a c-c-cyborg? Observe!"

His metal skull opened up, revealing a human-like brain pulsing inside. The brain floated above Honeycutt's head.

Casey leaned in for a closer look. "Dude! I wish I was a robot with a human brain!"

But Mikey had an ever *better* idea. "Ooh! What if we had *robot* brains?"

Mikey imagined himself flying through the air with a propeller-beanie on his head. Casey imagined himself as a tough, invulnerable robot with a huge blaster and a cool visor hiding his eyes.

Now firmly in the land of make-believe, both Mikey and Casey started doing stiff "robot" moves. *"Beetybeetybeety boop!"* Mikey said in his best robotic voice.

Raph smacked his forehead. "I just wish you guys had *normal* brains!"

Honeycutt sat in his cockpit chair. Metallic sides rose up around him, closing him in. "Everyone, hold on to something." This time, they all did. Mikey grabbed on to Casey.

"Actually," Honeycutt said, correcting himself, "you don't have to, because you won't feel any acceleration at this speed. We'll be converted into sentient plasma! Yes!"

Hanging on to each other, Mikey and Casey screamed, anticipating another painful journey. But when they looked out the spaceship's windows, all they saw was spectacular intergalactic beauty!

"Wow!" Leo said. "It's so incredible!"

"Look at that!" April said, pointing. "Are those comets?"

"So awesome . . . ," Mikey said.

Honeycutt joined them at the window. "Wondrous, is it not? Titanic gas giants, neutron stars on the verge of collapse, swirling cloud nebulas where baby stars are being born . . ."

"Aww," Mikey cooed. "Baby stars are so cute!"

As they marveled at the wonders of the galaxy, they were dealt a glancing blow by a small asteroid. A display popped up, indicating a minor leak.

"Aw, *beep*! Wonderful," Honeycutt sighed. "Could you assist me on damage assessment, my friends? I have plenty of space suits to wear!"

Mikey's eyes got stars in them! "*Space suits?* Dudes, I think we just hit a level-nine *booyakasha*!"

30

Honeycutt pressed a button, and the door to an airlock chamber slid open. The lights powered on.

The Turtles just stood there with their mouths hanging open.

"No way," Raph said. The chamber was full of space suits, gadgets, equipment, and even a few weapons!

The Turtles ran into the room.

"Amazing!" Donnie said, loading his arms up with gear. "This is like a full-on geek explosion!"

Smiling, Honeycutt made a sweeping gesture with his arm. "Astrosuits equipped with oxygen converters, grav boosters, and even alien language converters! *Beep!* And they glow in your appro-

priate colors because I sometimes have problems telling you apart. Heh heh heh."

As he spoke, the Turtles eagerly suited up, pulling on gloves, pants, jackets, boots, and helmets and striking heroic poses in their space suits.

"Mr. Crankshaw, set phasers to destruction!" Leo commanded in his best *Space Hero* voice.

Short wings flipped out of Mikey's tunic, startling him and setting him off balance. Windmilling his arms, he fell over. *WHOMP!*

Casey found an old-fashioned helmet. "Whoa, this old helmet is dope, yo!" When he picked it up, disk-shaped energy bombs fell on the floor. "Ooh, photon pucks! They must play hockey in space! Wicked!"

April zipped up a yellow jumpsuit and aimed a blaster.

"Wow . . . ," Donnie murmured.

"Looking good, Red!" Casey said enthusiastically.

April frowned. "Okay, you guys are creeping me out."

Professor Honeycutt stepped in front of the

door leading to the outside. "Everybody ready?"

April put on her helmet. They were ready. Honeycutt pressed a button and the door slid open. Beyond the open door . . . space.

"Do not stray too far from the ship," he continued. "Seriously. This is my stern face. See it?" He pointed to his face.

They stood there for a moment. Then Mikey cried out, "I call first!"

"No way! I'm first!" Raph argued. They struggled to get past each other. Mikey broke free and ran for the door. He leaped out into space, followed by the others. "*COWABUNGA!*"

The Teenage Mutant Ninja Turtles were in SPACE!